An ecosystem is a community of living things, like plants and animals, and nonliving things, like air, water, and soil, interacting as a system. In each ecosystem, special plants, animals, and fungi help maintain the conditions that support the system. Who are these caretakers?

Original Korean text by Eun-gyeong Gahng
Illustrations by Ji-eun Jeon
Korean edition © Aram Publishing

This English edition published by big & SMALL in 2016
by arrangement with Aram Publishing
English text edited by Joy Cowley
English edition © big & SMALL 2016

Distributed in the United States and Canada by
Lerner Publishing Group, Inc.
241 First Avenue North
Minneapolis, MN 55401 U.S.A.
www.lernerbooks.com

ISBN: 978-1-925247-15-2

Printed in Korea

The Best Caretakers

Written by Eun-gyeong Gahng
Illustrated by Ji-eun Jeon
Edited by Joy Cowley

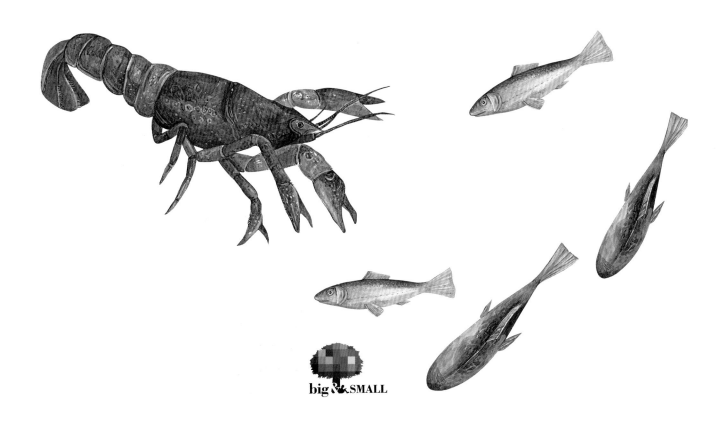

big & SMALL

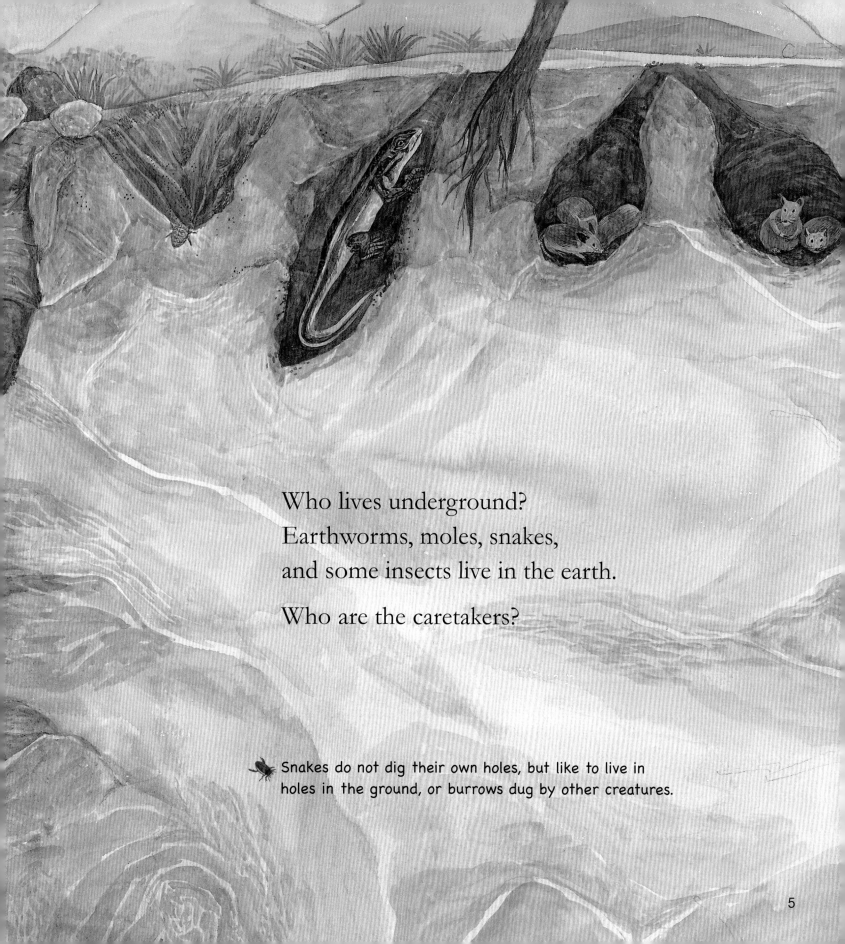

Who lives underground?
Earthworms, moles, snakes,
and some insects live in the earth.

Who are the caretakers?

Snakes do not dig their own holes, but like to live in
holes in the ground, or burrows dug by other creatures.

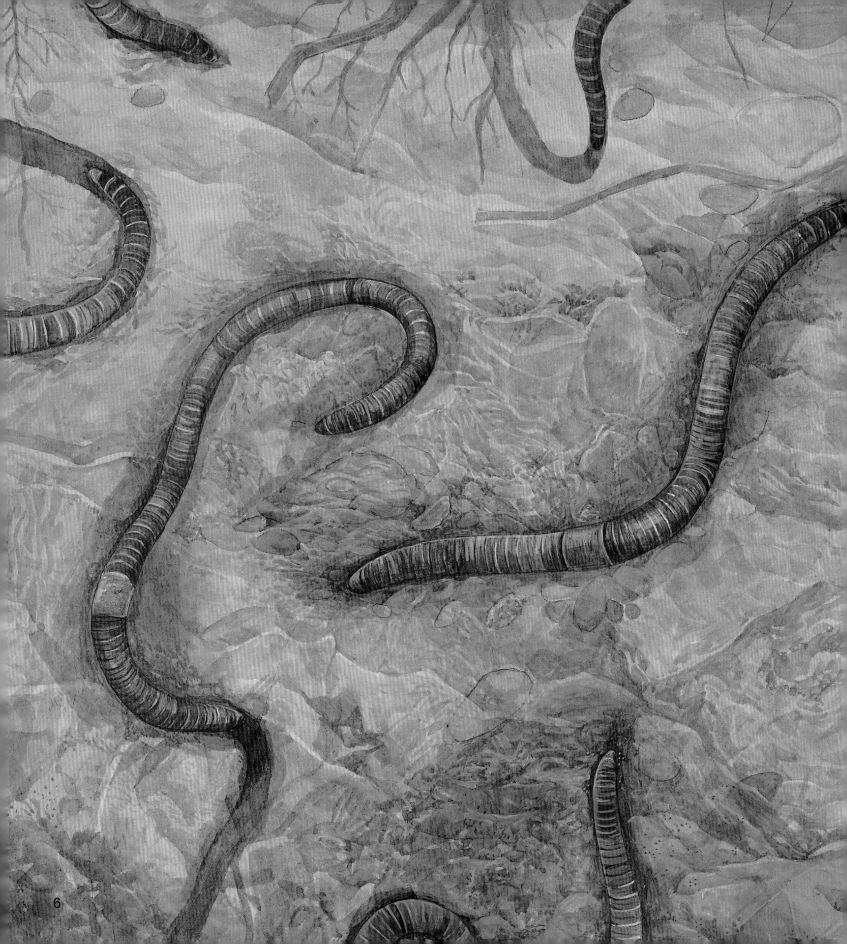

The earthworms are the caretakers.
They eat the remains
left by plants and animals.
Earthworms clean the soil.

When earthworms burrow in the soil,
they let air in for the roots of plants.
Earthworms eat the soil
and leave their dung behind.
The plants grow faster
with the nutrients in the dung.

Earthworms are sometimes known as 'ecosystem engineers' because they change the properties of soil.

Who lives in the forest?
Many animals, plants, and insects
live in the forest.

Among them are the caretakers.
Who are they?

The caretakers are mushrooms.
They grow using fallen leaves,
dead wood, and dead animals
for their nutrients.
Thanks to the mushrooms,
dead things don't pile up.

Mushrooms turn dead material
into good, rich soil.
Plants grow faster in the soil
that is made by mushrooms.
Mushrooms are the caretakers
in the forest.

Mushrooms are neither plants nor animals; they are fungi.

Who lives in the pond?
Animals and plants live there.

Who are the caretakers?

The caretakers are the water hyacinths.
They absorb dirty pond water
and grow fast and well.
Thanks to water hyacinths,
the water gets cleaner.

Who lives in the rivers?
Black snails, various fish,
and freshwater crayfish
live in the rivers.

Who are the caretakers?

The caretakers are black snails.
They eat dead fish and their dung.
They also eat green algae.
A black snail cleans
wherever it goes.
It is a good caretaker.

Who lives in the cities?
Many people and plants live in the cities.

Among them are caretakers.
Who are they?

The trees that line the streets
are the caretakers.
Smog from cars pollutes the air.
Trees turn polluted air
into fresh, clean air.
The more trees there are,
the cleaner the air in a city.

There are many caretakers living in this world.
They help support all the different ecosystems
by maintaining the conditions needed for life.

The Best Caretakers

An ecosystem is a community of living things, like plants and animals, and nonliving things, like air, water, and soil, interacting as a system. In each ecosystem, special plants, animals, and fungi help maintain the conditions that support the system. These plants and animals are the caretakers.

Let's think!

What is an ecosystem?

How do the caretakers help the ecosystem?

What would happen if the caretakers were not there?

Can humans be caretakers too?

Let's do!

You will need: paper, pencil, 12 feet of string, a small shovel or a spoon.

Go to a park or a natural area near you. Choose a site to observe. Take the string and mark out a 3 feet x 3 feet square. Use sticks or rocks to hold the string at the corners. This square is your ecosystem. Observe very closely what is within the boundaries of the ecosystem. Dig into parts of the soil so you can see underneath. Write down:

- The names of the nonliving things that are found within the square
- The names of the living things that are found within the square
- How do you think the living things relate to each other and to the nonliving things in that ecosystem?
- What would happen if one of the components was lost or reduced?